Watch *Postcards from Buster* on PBS!

From *Buster on the Town*, published by Little, Brown & Co. Copyright © 2005 Marc Brown

ISBN 0-316-15882-8 (hc) / 0-316-00107-4 (pb)

place
stamp
here

Watch *Postcards from Buster* on PBS!

From *Buster on the Town*, published by Little, Brown & Co. Copyright © 2005 Marc Brown

ISBN 0-316-15882-8 (hc) / 0-316-00107-4 (pb)

place
stamp
here

ILLINOIS

Name Means:
Men or Warriors

Nickname:
Prairie State

Capital:
Springfield

State Motto:
State Sovereignty,
National Union

Dear Arthur,
Did you know...

Buster on the Town

by Marc Brown

 LITTLE, BROWN AND COMPANY
New York ⚓ Boston

Copyright © 2005 by Marc Brown. All rights reserved.

Little, Brown and Company, Time Warner Book Group
1271 Avenue of the Americas, New York, NY 10020 • www.lb-kids.com
First Edition
Library of Congress Cataloging-in-Publication Data
Brown, Marc Tolon.
Buster on the town / Marc Brown.—1st ed.   p. cm.—(Postcards from Buster)
Summary: On his visit to Chicago, Buster makes a new friend and sends postcards back home.
ISBN 0-316-15882-8 (hc)/ISBN 0-316-00107-4 (pb)
[1. Postcards—Fiction. 2. Chicago (Ill.)—Fiction. 3. Rabbits—Fiction.] I. Title. II.
Series: Brown, Marc Tolon. Postcards from Buster. PZ7.B81618Bu 2005 [E]—dc22   2004010271

Printed in the United States of America • 10 9 8 7 6 5 4 3 2 1

Sears Tower pages 3 and 9: Sears Tower. Other photos from *Postcards from Buster* courtesy of WGBH Boston, and Cinar
Productions, Inc., in association with Marc Brown Studios.

Do you know what these words MEAN?

bakery: a place where bread and sweet things are made and sold

burfi, chum chum, and payta: Arabic words for kinds of sweet candy

Chicago (shi-KA-go): a large city in the state of **Illinois (il-ih-NOY)**

El: the abbreviation for elevated trains, the name of Chicago's subway system; some of the trains run above the streets.

Pakistan (PACK-ih-stan): a country in Asia

skyscraper: a very tall building

tower: a tall, narrow building

vegetables: plants with leaves, roots, or other parts that we eat

Chicago, Illinois

- The Sears Tower is the tallest building in the U.S.A.

- Chicago has the world's longest street (Western Ave).

- Chicago has the world's largest cookie factory (Nabisco).

Buster was busy
packing for a trip.

"I wish you could
take me," said Arthur.

"Sorry," said Buster.
"You won't fit
in my suitcase."

Chicago looked very tall
to Buster.

"So many skyscrapers,"
he said to his dad.
"It's confusing."

Dear Brain,

Did you know
the Sears Tower
has **2,232** stairs?

We took the elevator
to the Skydeck
on the 103rd floor.

Buster

CHICAGO
P.M.
OCT 4
2000
IL

United States
23¢

Alan "The Brain" Pow
22 Oak Street
Elwood City

↓ 103

CHICAGO

There were lots of people
at the top.

Buster met a girl named Farah.

"I'll bet you know
your way around,"
Buster said.

Dear Arthur,

This is Farah and her dad.

He is from Pakistan.

Farah was born in Chicago.

Buster

Arthur Read
100 Main Street
Elwood Cit

Buster went to a bakery
with Farah's family.

"This place reminds me
of the Sugar Bowl,"
said Buster.

Franc
Mapl
Elwo

Buster traveled
around the city
on the El.
There were
so many buildings
to keep track of.

Dear Brain,

I visited Farah's school.

They do the same math that we do.

It's easier when you only have to watch.

Buster

Alan "The Brain" Powers II
22 Oak Street
Elwood City

After school
they played basketball.

"Farah shoots! She scores!"
Buster shouted.

Binky Barnes
10 Pine Tre
Elwood Cit

23¢

Then Farah took Buster
to some stores.

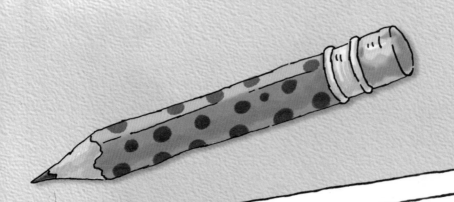

Dear Muffy,

I went shopping.
I saw some shoes
you would like.

Of course,
I've never seen shoes
you wouldn't like.

Buster

Muffy Crosswire
432 Valley View
Elwo

Finally, Buster had to say
goodbye to Farah.
"I think I'm finally
getting the hang
of this place."

Dear Farah,

Hope you can
visit me soon.

The Sugar Bowl
is waiting!

Buster